USBORNE BOOK OF CHILDREN'S CLASSICS

ROBINSON CRUSOE
TREASURE ISLAND
GULLIVER'S TRAVELS
KING ARTHUR

Retold by Angela Wilkes
Illustrated by Peter Dennis
Edited by Heather Amery

THE ADVENTURES OF
ROBINSON CRUSOE

By Daniel Defoe

Long ago in England there lived a boy called Robinson Crusoe. He wanted to be a sailor, but his father would not let him go to sea.

"You must stay at home and work hard," he said. Robinson decided that when he was older he would run away from home.

One day, a few years later, he was walking round a port when he met a friend who was going to sea. "Why don't you come?" said the friend.

Crusoe agreed to go at once. He was so excited, he forgot to send a message to his father. He boarded the ship and soon it set sail.

Crusoe never returned home. He sailed all round the world. Then he decided to live in Brazil, bought some land and planted tobacco.

He worked hard for many years. He sold the tobacco he grew and became a very rich man. But he still wanted to travel.

One day some friends asked him to go with them on a voyage to Africa to trade for gold and ivory. Crusoe was eager to go to sea again.

When their ship was ready Crusoe and his friends set sail. For twelve days the sea was calm, but then the wind began to blow hard.

Huge waves crashed over the ship's decks, snapping the masts and tearing the sails. The ship was caught in a hurricane. After a few days

it hit a sandbank. Fearing it might sink, the men decided to abandon ship. They lowered a boat and began to row away.

3

The wind blew harder and huge waves broke over the boat, filling it with water. The men pulled hard at the oars, hoping to reach land.

Suddenly the boat tilted and slid down the side of a gigantic wave. The boat turned over, throwing all the men into the water.

Crusoe felt himself sinking. He held his breath and swam to the surface. Then a wave lifted him and he saw land. He swam hard.

He had not gone far when the waves threw him against a rock. Crusoe clung to it. He waited for a break in the waves, then swam on.

At last he reached the bottom of a cliff. Panting, he climbed upwards. The waves crashed below him. Crusoe did not look down.

At the top of the cliff he sat down. "What will become of me?" he thought. All he had in his pockets was a knife, a pipe and tobacco.

Crusoe was very thirsty. He searched for fresh water and found a stream. It was getting dark, so he looked for a safe place to sleep.

He decided that in a tree he would be out of reach of wild animals. He chose one with spreading branches, climbed up and fell asleep.

Next morning Crusoe looked out from his tree. The tide had washed the ship nearer to the shore. "I shall go out to it," thought Crusoe.

He climbed down from the tree and went to the beach. There he found some shoes and a hat. They were the only signs of his friends.

"I'm alone, but lucky to be alive," Crusoe thought sadly. "But how long shall I survive here?" He decided to swim out to the ship.

The ship was not far off. But when Crusoe reached it he found it lay high out of the water and he did not know how to climb aboard.

He swam round the ship and saw a rope hanging down. After a struggle Crusoe caught hold of it and pulled himself up on to the ship.

He went straight to the store room. All the food was still dry. Crusoe opened a box of biscuits. He was very hungry.

Next he decided to make a raft to carry things back to the shore. He collected big pieces of wood and threw them into the sea.

He had tied the pieces of wood to the ship so they would not float away. He pulled them closer and climbed down on to them.

He lashed four lengths of wood together, then tied more pieces across them. This made his raft strong enough to walk on.

6

Crusoe loaded the raft with the most useful things he could find – chests full of food, barrels of rum, guns and barrels of gunpowder.

Then, using a pole as a steering pole, he guided the raft towards the shore. He landed it on the beach and unloaded his cargo.

After eating some of the food, Crusoe climbed a hill to see where he was. At the top he looked round and saw he was on an island.

The next day he returned to the ship and collected more tools and clothes. To his delight, he also found the ship's dog and two cats.

Crusoe went back to the ship every day and soon had many useful things. He piled them up round a tent he had made from poles and sails.

One night there was another fierce storm. When Crusoe looked out of his tent the next morning, he saw that the ship had been washed away.

Crusoe looked for somewhere to live. He wanted to be near a stream and to have a view of the sea in case a ship ever passed by.

He soon found a good place. It was a flat space up on a hill facing the sea. At the back was a steep cliff with a cave at the bottom of it.

First Crusoe built a fence. He cut up wood to make posts and drove them into the ground in a semi-circle in front of the cave.

Before finishing the fence, he carried his stores up to the cave. When the fence was complete he made a ladder so he could climb over it.

Inside the fence Crusoe set up a large tent of wood and sails he had saved from the ship. First he made a small tent, then he built a bigger one over it, to protect it from the rain. This was to be his home. But as he also wanted a dry store room, he decided to enlarge the cave.

First he needed a spade. He found a tree with very hard wood and cut off a branch. Then he carefully carved it into the shape of a spade.

To make the cave bigger, he dug out earth and sand. He piled the earth against the inside of the fence to make it stronger.

During the next few weeks Crusoe made his cave more comfortable. He made a table and a chair from planks he had saved from the ship.

He had never done any carpentry before but he found that if he worked slowly he could manage to make anything he wanted.

Crusoe soon settled down to life on the island. Every morning he went out hunting with his dog, to shoot birds or wild goats for food.

Sometimes he climbed the cliffs to look for seabirds' nests in cracks in the rocks. The birds flew round as he collected the eggs.

At mid-day he went home and cooked his food over a fire. He skinned all the animals he caught or shot and dried the skins to use later.

It was too hot to work in the afternoons, so Crusoe slept in a hammock he had made, tied between two poles in his tent.

Later, when it was cooler, he started work again on more things for the cave. Everything took him a long time but he did not mind.

In the evenings Crusoe wrote his diary. He lit the cave with candles he had made, which were wicks floating in dishes of goat's fat.

Crusoe did not want to lose count of the days while he was on the island, so he made a sort of calendar with a pole he set up on the beach.

Every day he cut a notch in the pole. For Sundays and the first day of a month he cut longer notches, so that he always knew the date.

One day Crusoe shook out an old corn sack he found among his things. There was very little corn left in it and he wanted to use the sack.

Months later he found ripe corn growing. Crusoe picked it and kept the grain to plant later, so he could grow enough corn for bread.

One day, when Crusoe was in his cave, the ground shook and rocks crashed down the cliff. Terrified, Crusoe ran outside. It was an earthquake. When it was over, a huge storm blew up. Crusoe crept back to his cave. He felt very lucky to be still alive.

When Crusoe had been on the island for ten months he set off to explore it. He took his gun in case he met any savages or wild animals.

In the middle of the island, he came to a green valley where orange trees grew. "I will build a home here one day," he thought.

Vines heavy with grapes grew in the valley. Crusoe picked as many grapes as he could carry. Later he dried them in the sun to make raisins.

There were many parrots in that part of the island. Crusoe knocked a young one down from a tree and took it home with him.

He made the parrot a perch and spent hours teaching it to talk. After a while it could say "Robinson" and its own name, "Poll".

One day Crusoe shot a baby goat by mistake. He took it home to look after it and it became tame. Crusoe now had several pets.

Just before the rainy season Crusoe planted his corn. Soon he had a fine cornfield. He built a fence round it to keep out the wild goats.

Then birds began to peck at the corn. Crusoe shot a few and hung them on posts round the field to scare away away other birds.

Crusoe needed something to keep his corn in, so he made pots from clay and dried them in the sun. The first ones were not very round.

One day a pot fell in the fire. Then Crusoe found that if he baked his pots they would hold water and he could use them for cooking.

When Crusoe had cut his corn he was ready to make bread. He ground the corn into flour, then mixed it with water to make a dough.

He put loaves of dough on to tiles and covered them with bowls. He laid them in hot ashes to cook, and soon he had baked his first loaves.

One day, as Crusoe was exploring the island, he came to some high cliffs. He looked out to sea and, to his surprise, saw land on the horizon. He did not know if it was the mainland or another island. Suddenly he felt lonely and wanted to escape from his island.

He went to look at a boat which had been washed ashore in a storm. He tried to push it down to the sea but it was too heavy.

He decided to make himself a boat like an Indian canoe. He went into the woods and chose a straight tree growing on the edge of the beach.

He cut it down and trimmed off the branches. This took him a long time. Then he hollowed out the trunk, using tools from the ship.

After many weeks the canoe was finished. It was huge. Crusoe was proud of it. "It is big enough to carry all my stores," he thought.

But Crusoe had built his boat a long way from the sea and he could not move it. He began to dig a canal so he could float it down to the sea, but he soon realised it would take him years. All his work was wasted. Sadly he stopped digging and gave up any idea of escape.

Crusoe had now been on the island for four years and his clothes were in rags. He had no cloth for new ones but he had plenty of goatskins.

He had stretched all the goatskins over sticks and hung them up to dry. He sewed them together to make trousers, a jerkin and a hat.

The new clothes looked very odd, but Crusoe was pleased with them. They protected him from the fierce sun and the tropical rain.

Crusoe also made an umbrella. He used sticks for the frame and goatskins for the cover. On hot days he used it as a sunshade.

Crusoe still wanted a boat and after a while he made another one. It was smaller than the first one and this time he built it by the sea.

Crusoe knew he could not sail to the mainland. The boat was too small for that. He just wanted to sail all round the island.

When he had finished the boat, Crusoe stocked it with food for the voyage – loaves of bread, meat, raisins and water.

He fixed his umbrella up at the back of the boat to shade him from the hot sun and he put his gun in a safe place. Then he set sail.

The sun was shining and there was a good breeze to fill the sail. Crusoe steered along the coast, carefully avoiding rocks.

He stopped in a small bay and went ashore. He climbed a hill to look around and noticed there were dangerous currents out at sea.

Crusoe set off again, staying close to the shore. But he had not gone far when the boat was suddenly caught in a strong current.

Crusoe lowered the sail and struggled to row against the current, but it was no use. He was being swept far out to sea.

Suddenly the wind changed. Crusoe put up his sail and found that he was being blown out of the current and back towards the island.

When he reached the coast, he staggered ashore and fell on his knees to thank God he was safe. Then he walked back across the island.

As soon as he was home, he climbed into his hammock and fell asleep. Suddenly he was woken up by a voice calling his name. Frightened,

he grabbed his gun and sat up. Then he laughed. Perched in front of him was his parrot. "Poor Robin Crusoe," it squawked cheerfully.

Pole I set up on the beach to mark the other side of the island

Beach where there are many turtles

My country home

Cove where I keep my boat

High cliffs from which I can see land

Paddock where I keep my goats

Look-out point

Stream

My cornfield

My fortress

Calendar pole

The cliff I first climbed

Sandbank on which the ship was wrecked

My raft

The rocks I was swept on to

This is the map of the island that Crusoe drew after he had sailed round it.

He marked on it all the places he knew and added more as he went exploring.

Dangerous currents out at sea

Rocky point

first
t I
de

N
W — E
S

After he had been on the island for a few years, Crusoe built a summer home in the valley where the orange trees grew.

He made a tent and planted young trees round it. They grew fast and gave plenty of shade. It was a cool place to spend hot summer days.

Crusoe kept his goats in a paddock next to his summer home. He caught his first goats in a pit trap and soon tamed them.

They had kids and after a year Crusoe had a whole flock of goats. He milked them and made butter and cheese from their milk.

Crusoe had been on the island for twelve years and was quite content. He had all he wanted and felt like the king of the island.

Then one day he saw a foot print on the beach. He stopped, listened and stared all round him but he could not hear or see anyone.

Terrified, he ran home. He dared not look back. He was sure he was being followed and that savages were lurking behind every bush.

He hid in his fortress for days, too scared to come out. Then he wondered if he was being silly. "Perhaps it is my foot print," he thought.

He went back to the beach and measured his foot against the print. The print was larger. A stranger must have been on the island.

Crusoe rushed home. He made his fence stronger and fixed guns in it. He planted trees round his fortress so they would grow and hide it.

Another year passed and Crusoe did not see anyone. Then one morning, as he walked along a beach, he stopped in horror. On the ground were the remains of a fire and round it were human bones. Crusoe felt sick. Cannibals, man-eating savages, had been there.

Crusoe did not feel safe any more. He was sure the cannibals would return. He found a hiding place and looked out to sea every day.

One day, when he was cutting wood, he found a cave. "No one would find my guns and gunpowder here," he thought.

He walked into the cave, then ran out in fright. Two eyes were shining at him out of the darkness. Perhaps it was a cannibal.

Crusoe plucked up his courage. He lit a torch and went back into the cave. Then he laughed. "It's only a poor old goat," he said.

Months went by and Crusoe did not see any savages. Then early one morning he saw the light of a fire on the beach. He ran home.

He loaded his guns in case the cannibals found his corn field and came looking for him. But he wanted to know what was going on.

He crept back to the beach to watch. Nine savages were dancing round a fire and feasting. When they had finished, they got into

their canoes and paddled away towards the mainland. Crusoe was glad to see them go. From then on he looked out for them every day.

One night after this there was a bad storm. Crusoe was in his cave, reading a book he had found on the ship. Suddenly he heard a gunshot.

He knew he could not help the people on the ship, but hoped they might be able to rescue him. He lit a fire on the cliffs as a beacon.

But when day broke, he saw the ship was wrecked. His heart sank. He could not escape now. He hoped there would be some survivors.

He ran out to the look-out point on the cliff. A flash of lightning lit the sky and Crusoe saw a ship tossing on the stormy seas.

He sailed out to the wreck but, to his dismay, found that there was no one alive on board. He would have to remain alone on the island.

Most of the ship's cargo had been spoiled by sea water. Crusoe found a chest full of gold. "What use is gold to me?" he asked himself sadly.

Suddenly the second captive broke away from the group and ran away towards the woods. Two of the cannibals chased after him.

Two years went by peacefully, then Crusoe saw five canoes on the beach near his home. He crept closer to look. About thirty savages were roasting meat over a fire and two captives were waiting to be killed. As Crusoe watched, the savages hit one captive on the head.

Crusoe ran home and fetched his guns. He wanted to save the captive. "He could keep me company," he thought and hurried back to the beach.

As soon as the three savages were out of sight of the cannibals on the beach, Crusoe ran out towards them. They stopped, surprised by this man in goatskins. Crusoe ran up to one of the pursuers and hit him so hard on the head with his gun that he fell down dead.

The second savage pulled back his bow to shoot, but Crusoe was too quick for him. He fired his gun and killed him instantly.

The captive stopped running when he saw his enemies were dead and stared at Crusoe. Crusoe smiled and beckoned, to show he was friendly.

The captive slowly came forwards, then knelt and kissed the ground at Crusoe's feet. This meant he wanted to be Crusoe's servant.

After burying the savages in the sand, Crusoe took the man home with him. He gave him food, then the tired savage fell asleep.

25

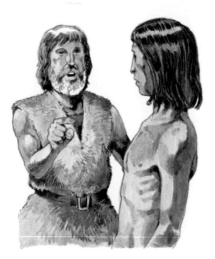

Next day Crusoe began to teach the savage English. He taught him his name was Friday, as that was the day on which he had been saved.

Crusoe and Friday went to the beach. The cannibals had gone. Friday pointed to the graves. He wanted to dig up the savages and eat them.

Crusoe was very angry. He tried to show that the thought of eating people made him feel sick. Friday understood and looked sad.

Back at the fortress, Crusoe gave Friday some clothes. Friday was proud of them, but felt uncomfortable. He had not worn clothes before.

Crusoe decided to teach Friday to eat animal meat. He took him hunting with him and shot a goat. The noise of the gun scared Friday.

He looked at his stomach to see if he had been hurt. He did not understand how the gun had killed the goat. He begged Crusoe not to kill him.

26

As time passed, Crusoe taught Friday to fire a gun, to help in the cornfield and to make bread. Friday was quick to learn.

He learned English and he and Crusoe told each other about their homes. Crusoe was glad to have someone to talk to at long last.

One clear day Friday saw the mainland. He was excited. "Look," he called to Crusoe, "There is my home. Let us make a boat and go there."

"I can't go," said Crusoe. "Your cannibal friends will eat me." "No," said Friday, "They will like you because you saved my life."

So Crusoe and Friday made a boat and Crusoe taught Friday how to sail it. They collected food for their voyage to the mainland.

Then one day Friday saw three canoes approaching the shore. The cannibals were back. Terrified, Friday ran to tell Crusoe.

"We must fight them," said Crusoe. He and Friday loaded the guns and shared out the weapons. Then they crept down to a wood by the beach.

Friday climbed a tree to see what was happening. Many savages were feasting round a fire. They had one captive. It was a white man.

Crusoe and Friday hid in the bushes near the beach. "Fire!" shouted Crusoe and they shot at the savages, killing some and wounding others.

The ones who were not hurt were terrified. They sprang to their feet but did not know where to run. Crusoe and Friday fired again.

Then they rushed out of the bushes. The savages ran towards the canoes, hoping to escape, but Friday chased them, firing his gun.

Crusoe ran to the captive and untied him. The captive was a Spaniard. Crusoe gave him a gun and told him to try and defend himself.

Soon they had killed all the savages except for three, who escaped in a canoe. "Quick," Crusoe shouted to Friday, "We must stop them."

He ran to a canoe and, to his surprise, found an old man lying in it, tied and gagged. As Crusoe untied him, Friday ran up to him.

When Friday saw the old man he shouted for joy, then rushed over to him and hugged him. "This is my father," he told Crusoe.

Friday's father and the Spanish captive were weak. Crusoe and Friday carried them back to the fortress so they could eat and rest.

The next day the Spaniard told Crusoe that there were more Spanish sailors on the mainland. "I must go back to them," he told Crusoe.

Crusoe gave him food and weapons and soon the Spaniard set sail for the mainland, taking Friday's father with him.

A week later, to his surprise, Crusoe saw an English ship moored off the coast. He wondered why it had come to the island.

Looking through his telescope, he saw a boat full of sailors coming in to land. Three of the sailors were prisoners.

The sailors left the boat on the beach and went off to explore the island, leaving the three prisoners tied up under a tree.

Crusoe and Friday walked down to the beach and went up to the prisoners. "Who are you?" Crusoe asked them gently. "Can we help you?"

The prisoners stared at Crusoe. "I was the captain of that ship," one said. "My sailors mutinied and are leaving us on this island."

"I will help you," said Crusoe, "if you take us to England after we recapture your ship." The captain agreed and Crusoe untied him.

As the sailors returned to the beach, they were seized. Crusoe told them that he would spare their lives if they swore to help him.

Soon more sailors came ashore. Seeing the boat but no one on the beach, they called out. Crusoe told Friday to lure them away.

Friday hid in the trees and answered the sailors' calls. Thinking he was one of their friends, they went looking for him and got lost.

As they looked for the way back to the beach, the captain's men ambushed them, tied them up and led them to Crusoe's fortress.

When it was dark, the captain rowed out to the ship with twelve trusted men. They quietly climbed aboard, then opened fire.

Taken by surprise, the rebels surrendered. The captain then fired a signal to let Crusoe know that the ship had been recaptured.

Next morning the captain rowed back to Crusoe. "The ship is yours," he said. Crusoe was delighted. At last he could leave the island.

The captain had presents for Crusoe, who put on his first proper clothes for many years. Then he, Friday and the captain had a great feast.

Robinson Crusoe was written by Daniel Defoe in 1720. It is based on the adventures of a sailor called Alexander Selkirk, who was cast away on a desert island and lived there for five years before he was rescued.

Defoe took the idea of being shipwrecked on a desert island and turned it into a moving survival story. He shows how Robinson Crusoe makes a success of his life on the island by his determination and common sense, and by making good use of whatever he finds.

Daniel Defoe (1660-1731) lived in London and started his career as a business man. He wrote political pamphlets and was put in prison for a while for attacking the government. He did not start writing fiction until he was sixty. *Robinson Crusoe* was his first novel and this was followed by *Moll Flanders* and *A Journal of the Plague Year*.

They set sail for home and, after a long journey, finally reached England. Crusoe had been away thirtyfive years. The gold he had saved from

the wreck made him a very rich man. Friday stayed with him for the rest of his days and they never forgot their life on the desert island.

TREASURE ISLAND

By Robert Louis Stevenson

He stopped at the inn. "Many people here?" he asked. Jim shook his head. "Then this is the place for me," said the captain.

Long ago a boy called Jim Hawkins lived alone with his mother on a wild stretch of English coast. She kept the "Admiral Benbow" inn.

One windy day a sea captain came up the road, singing a shanty, "Fifteen men on the dead man's chest! Yo ho ho and a bottle of rum!"

He gave Jim a silver coin. "I'll give you a coin every month if you keep a sharp look-out for a sailor with only one leg," he said.

The captain's name was Billy Bones. He soon became well known at the inn for the dreadful stories he told about wicked pirates.

He stayed at the inn for month after month but never paid Jim's mother any money. She was too scared of him to ask for it.

One winter's morning, when Billy Bones was out, a stranger came to the inn. "Is there a captain staying here?" he asked.

Suddenly he saw Billy Bones coming along the road. He pushed Jim into the inn and dragged him behind a door. "Keep quiet," he hissed.

Jim was very scared. Billy Bones came in and walked across the room. "Good day to you, Captain," growled the stranger.

Billy Bones spun round. His face went pale and he looked as if he had seen a ghost. "You remember me, don't you?" asked the stranger.

35

"You are Black Dog," gasped Billy Bones. "Yes," said the stranger. "We have business to discuss." They sent Jim for some rum.

Suddenly Jim heard shouts and the sound of chairs being knocked over. He ran back into the room. The men were drawing their swords.

Billy Bones lunged at Black Dog, then chased him out of the inn. Black Dog fled, blood pouring from a wound in his shoulder.

Suddenly Billy Bones gasped and clutched his chest. He was having a heart attack. He fell to the ground and Jim ran to help him.

Bones had to stay in bed after his attack. He called Jim. "You must help me," he whispered. "Cap'n Flint's pirates are after me."

"They want something I've hidden in my seaman's chest. If ever you see any strangers around, you must call the law at once."

Time went by and Jim saw no suspicious strangers. Then one cold, foggy day he saw a hunched old man coming slowly up the road.

The man was blind and tapped the road with a stick. When he reached the inn he stopped and called out, "Where am I?"

"At the 'Admiral Benbow' inn," said Jim. The blind man grabbed his hand. "Take me to Billy Bones," he hissed fiercely.

Frightened, Jim led him inside. "Here's a friend come to see you, Captain Bones," he said. Billy Bones looked up in terror.

"Hold out your hand," said the blind man. He hobbled up to the captain, pressed a note into his hand and hurried out of the inn.

Bones read the note. "The pirates are coming at ten," he said. He jumped up but suddenly gasped and fell down. He was dead.

37

Jim and his mother were scared about the pirates coming to the inn. But Jim's mother wanted to find Billy Bones' money.

They ran to the village to ask for help. But everyone was too scared of pirates to go back to the "Admiral Benbow" with them.

So Jim and his mother crept home on their own. When they reached the inn they rushed inside and locked all the doors and windows.

Then they looked for Billy Bones' money. Jim found a key round Bones' neck. "This could be the key to the chest in his room," he said.

He and his mother ran upstairs to Bones' room. The key fitted the chest, so they quickly unlocked it and threw open the lid.

The chest was full of odd things – clothes, trinkets and pistols. Underneath Jim found a packet of papers and a heavy bag.

The bag was full of money. "I'll take what I'm owed," said Jim's mother, and they began to count the coins. Suddenly they stopped. Some one was rattling the door of the inn. Then they heard the blind man's stick tap down the road. "Quick," said Jim. "We must go."

They took the money and papers and fled from the inn. Then Jim heard people coming. He pulled his mother into a hiding place.

A band of men broke down the inn door. As they ran through the house Jim heard shouts of "Bones is dead" and "Find his chest!"

Suddenly the blind man threw open the window of Billy Bones' room. "The papers have gone!" he shrieked. "Find the boy!"

The pirates searched the whole inn for Jim, then met outside. Suddenly they heard a whistle. "The warning!" one of them cried and they raced towards the cliffs. A group of soldiers galloped over the hill. They had heard that Jim and his mother were in danger.

The pirates ran to a cove where a boat was waiting. The soldiers chased after them but they were too late The pirates had escaped.

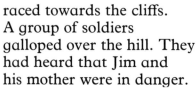

"The pirates were looking for this packet of papers," Jim told the captain of the soldiers. "We should take it to Squire Trelawny."

The captain took Jim to the Hall, where Squire Trelawny was dining with Dr. Livesey. They were very surprised to hear Jim's story.

Dr. Livesey opened the packet. In it was a map of an island. Next to a cross on it was written: "Most of treasure here."

The Map of the Island

The map showed that the island was nine miles long and five miles wide.

It had two sheltered inlets and a hill in the middle, called "The Spy Glass".

"This shows where Captain Flint's treasure is buried," he said. "No wonder Flint's crew were after Billy Bones. They wanted this map!"

The squire was excited. "I'll find a ship and crew and we will sail to the island," he said. "But we mustn't tell anyone about the treasure."

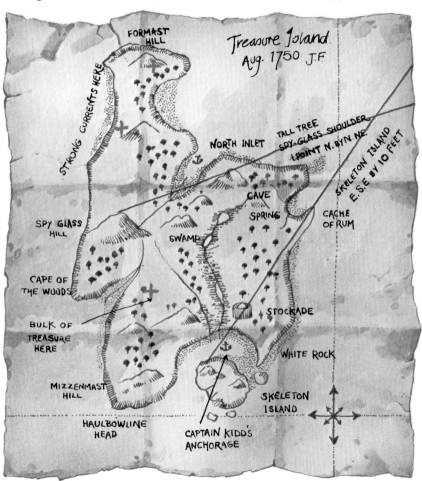

On the back of the map was more writing:

The silver is in the northern hiding place. Follow the east hill ten fathoms south of the black rock with a face on it.

The weapons are buried beneath the sand dune on the north point of the north inlet cape bearing E and a quarter N.

A month later Jim said goodbye to his mother and left the inn. He went to Bristol and met Squire Trelawny at the harbour.

"There's our ship," said the squire, pointing. "She's called the *Hispaniola*. I've picked a good crew for her and we sail tomorrow."

Jim had to take a message to the landlord of a nearby inn. He was called Long John Silver and he was to be the new ship's cook.

Long John was friendly, but Jim saw that he only had one leg. "Bones told me about him," he thought, "but he's too nice to be a pirate."

42

Jim went back to the squire and found Dr. Livesey with him. They rowed out to the *Hispaniola*. They were very excited about the voyage.

On board they met Captain Smollett, the ship's captain. "I thought everything about this voyage was to be kept a secret," he said angrily.

"Now I find that all the crew know exactly where we are going and that you are after Flint's treasure. I don't trust any of them."

The squire and Dr. Livesey were worried to hear this, but it was too late to find a new crew. The next day the *Hispaniola* set sail.

Jim soon became friends with Long John. Long John had a parrot he called Cap'n Flint, after the famous pirate who had died.

One night Jim went on deck and climbed into a barrel to fetch an apple. Suddenly he heard men near him talking very quietly.

It was Long John whispering to a sailor. "I was Cap'n Flint's right-hand man," he said. "All his crew were afraid of me."

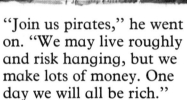

"Join us pirates," he went on. "We may live roughly and risk hanging, but we make lots of money. One day we will all be rich."

"This voyage seems much more exciting now," said the sailor, "I'll join you." Long John laughed wickedly and they shook hands on it.

Jim was horrified. Captain Smollett had been right not to trust the crew. They were plotting mutiny. How many of them were pirates?

A third man came along. It was Long John's friend, Israel Hands. "How long are we going to wait before we strike?" he grumbled.

"We'll wait until we have the treasure," said Long John, "then we'll kill the captain and all the loyal members of his crew."

Just then the moon rose and there was a cry of "Land ahoy!" Everyone rushed on to the deck. An island loomed in the distance.

"Have any of you been here before?" asked the captain. "I want to know a safe place to anchor." "I've been here, sir," said Long John.

The captain showed him a chart. Long John looked at it eagerly, but the treasure was not marked on it. He pointed to an inlet.

While the crew were busy, Jim went up to the doctor. "I must talk to you in private," he whispered. "I have some terrible news."

The doctor hurried away. A few minutes later Jim was called to the captain's cabin. He told his friends what he had heard.

"It's too late to turn back now," said the captain. "We must find out how many men are on our side and be ready for trouble."

The next morning the
Hispaniola anchored in a
wooded inlet. It was very
hot and the island looked
gloomy and forbidding.

The men had to work hard
all day and were grumbling.
Long John looked worried.
Captain Smollett was afraid
that the crew would rebel.

He called them together.
"It's been a hot day and
you are tired," he said.
"You can take the afternoon
off and go ashore."

The men cheered and ran to
the boats. Jim decided he
wanted to go ashore too.
When no one was looking, he
slipped into one of the boats.

Jim's boat was the first to
reach the island and Jim
jumped ashore. Long John
called out after him but
Jim pretended not to hear
and ran into the trees.

"Join us pirates," he hissed. The sailor shook his head. Suddenly they heard a scream. It sounded as if someone was being killed.

The sailor jumped. "So you are murdering people now," he said. "Well, I dare you to kill me too." Bravely he turned to walk away.

He was exploring the island when he heard footsteps. He hid behind a bush and peered out into a clearing. Long John was talking to one of the sailors.

Long John whipped the crutch from under his arm and hurled it at the sailor. It hit him so hard, he fell down dead instantly.

Jim was terrified. He did not wait to see what happened next but ran as fast as he could from the scene of the murder.

47

Jim ran for a long time, then a sudden noise made him stop. He looked round and saw a shadowy figure dodge behind a tree.

Jim's heart jumped. What was following him? Was it a man or a bear? He felt in his pocket for a gun and crept towards the tree.

Suddenly a wild man stepped out and knelt down. "Don't shoot, I'm poor Ben Gunn," he said. "I haven't spoken to a soul for three years."

"My pirate friends left me here to die," he went on, "but I'm still alive and now I'm rich. What are you doing here?" he asked Jim.

Jim told him what had happened. "Tell the squire I can help him and make him rich if he helps me to escape from here," said Ben.

Just then they heard the sound of a cannon. "I must go back," said Jim. He and Ben ran to where the ship was anchored.

Meanwhile, back on the ship, the doctor found Jim was missing and was worried. He rowed ashore with one of the men to look for him.

Not far inland they came to a stockade, a log house surrounded by a strong fence. The house was on a hill and could be easily defended.

Suddenly they too heard the scream. "The trouble has begun," said the doctor. "We must fetch the others and barricade ourselves in here."

They returned to the ship and loaded a boat with guns. They set off for the shore but the boat was overloaded and began to sink.

There were some pirates left on the ship and they loaded the cannon. The squire shot at them and they fired the cannon.

The squire's men reached the shore safely and ran for the stockade. Long John's men on the island heard the firing and chased after them.

As Jim ran to the ship he heard the gunfire and saw the Jolly Roger, the pirate's flag, flying from the mast. Then he saw the captain's

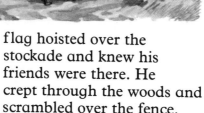

flag hoisted over the stockade and knew his friends were there. He crept through the woods and scrambled over the fence.

The doctor and the squire were pleased to see him. Jim told them about Long John killing the sailor and about meeting Ben Gunn.

Jim's friends looked grim. They did not have many guns. They decided to stay in the stockade for the night and fight the pirates.

Next day there was a cry of "Flag of Truce." To everyone's surprise, Long John was hobbling up the hill, waving a white flag.

"I'll make a deal," he told the captain. "Give us the chart and stop shooting and we'll let you on the ship and take you to a port."

"I'll not bargain," said the captain. "Surrender and I'll take you home to a fair trial. Otherwise we fight on." Silver limped angrily away.

When he had gone, the captain gave orders to prepare to fight. The men took up positions and waited. It was a very hot day.

Suddenly shots rang out and a band of pirates ran out of the woods towards the stockade. As they swarmed over the fence, the squire's men opened fire.

In the fierce battle that followed, both pirates and loyal sailors were killed. Suddenly the fighting was over and the last pirates fled into the woods.

The squire walked round inside the stockade. Five pirates and two of his men had been killed, and Captain Smollett was badly wounded.

Dr. Livesey bound the captain's wounds. Then he took the chart and went into the woods. "He's gone to find Ben," thought Jim.

Jim could not bear the sight of the dead and wounded. When no one was looking, he took two pistols and slipped away into the woods.

He wanted to look for a boat Ben Gunn had built. He walked quietly down to the shore and saw Long John rowing away from the ship.

He crept along the beach until he found a big white rock Ben had told him about. Hidden beneath it was a small goatskin tent.

Jim lifted a corner of the tent and found Ben Gunn's boat there. It was a coracle, a round boat made of thick sticks and goatskins.

Now Jim had a new idea. He decided to paddle out to the ship and cut it adrift. He lifted the coracle and took it down to the water.

He launched it into the waves and got in, but found it hard to steer. When he tried to paddle, the boat just spun round and round.

But luckily the tide swept the coracle towards the *Hispaniola*. Soon Jim saw it looming up out of the darkness in front of him.

Jim came alongside the ship and caught hold of the anchor rope. Slowly he cut through it. Suddenly he heard shouting on board.

He lifted himself up to a porthole and looked inside. Israel Hands and another of the pirates were struggling in a terrible fight.

The ship began to turn and Jim dropped back into the coracle. He was very tired and fell asleep as the coracle drifted out to sea.

When Jim woke up he felt hot and dazed. It was already day and the coracle was tossing on the waves off the coast of the island.

There was a line of jagged rocks between Jim and the beach, so he paddled on, hoping to land his boat further along the coast.

Suddenly, right in front of him, Jim saw the *Hispaniola* skimming across the waves. All at once she turned and her sails went slack.

No one seemed to be steering her. Jim wondered where the sailors were and paddled towards the ship, hoping to board her and take her over.

Again the ship turned and headed straight for him. Just as the ship crushed the tiny boat, Jim sprang up and caught hold of the boom.

One sailor was dead. The other one groaned and Jim ran to his side. It was Israel Hands. "What are you doing here?" he muttered.

"I'm taking command of the ship and sailing her to the captain," said Jim. "Give me food and drink and I'll help you," said Hands slyly.

He swung himself on to the ship and looked round. To his horror, he saw two sailors lying in pools of blood on the deck.

Jim took down the Jolly Roger and threw it overboard. Then he bandaged Hands' wounds and they sailed for the northern inlet.

When they got there they had to wait a while for the tide to turn. "Will you go below and fetch me some wine?" asked Hands craftily.

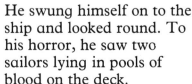

Jim did not trust Hands. He went below, ran to the far end of the ship and looked out. He saw Hands crawl across the deck to some rope and take out a long, rusty dagger. Hands felt its blade, then hid it under his jacket and crawled back to his place. Jim had seen enough.

He took Hands some wine and Hands swigged it down, pretending to be very weak. "We'll sail the ship in now," he whispered hoarsely to Jim.

As Jim was sailing the ship into the inlet, a sudden noise made him turn. Hands was behind him, knife in hand, ready to strike him.

He lunged at Jim, but Jim nimbly leapt to one side and Hands hit his chest on the tiller, which winded him for a few seconds.

Jim quickly took out his pistols. He aimed and tried to fire them, but there was only a dull click. He had forgotten to load them.

Hands threw himself at Jim
again and Jim dodged
behind a mast. Hands chased
Jim round the ship, but Jim
was too quick for him.

Suddenly the ship tilted and
Jim and Hands were thrown
on to the deck. Jim leapt
to his feet. He had to find
a new way of escape.

He sprang up the mast
ropes, but Hands slowly
hauled himself up after him.
Terrified, Jim loaded the
pistols. "Come no further
or I'll shoot," he cried.

Suddenly Hands threw the
dagger and it pinned Jim's
shoulder to the mast. As Jim
cried out with pain, the
pistols went off. Hands
screamed and fell into the sea.

Jim clung to the mast. His shoulder was very painful. Bravely he pulled the dagger out and climbed shakily back down to the deck.

He slipped overboard into the shallow water and waded ashore. "Now the ship is ready for the captain again," he thought happily.

He set off across the island towards the stockade to look for his friends. As he came near the house he could see the glow of a big fire.

He crept into the house. No one was on watch and Jim could not see in the dark. "Pieces of eight," a shrill voice suddenly called out.

It was Long John's parrot. "Who's there?" called Long John. Jim turned to run but someone grabbed him and held up a light.

"Look who's here," said Long John. "You'll have to join us now. Your friends have given you up and gone away. Or would you rather die?"

"I don't have much choice," said Jim bravely, "but if you spare me I will help you when you return to England and are tried for piracy."

Snarling, one of the pirates drew his knife and sprang at Jim, but Long John stopped him. "I give the orders round here," he said.

The pirate stepped back and the others gathered round him. "Let's go outside," said one and they went out, muttering angrily.

"I'm in trouble," Long John whispered to Jim. "The ship has gone. But at least the doctor gave me the chart." Jim was astonished.

The pirates came back. One of them stepped forward. "We want a new leader," he said. Long John said nothing, but held up the chart.

The pirates whooped joyfully. They had not known about the chart. They passed it round, shouting, "We'll be rich after all!"

59

Next day Dr. Livesey walked into the stockade. He had come to tend to the wounded pirates. He was very surprised to see Jim.

Jim apologised to him for deserting his friends and told him where the ship was. "Don't worry," said the doctor. "We'll save you."

He went over to Long John. "There'll be trouble when you look for the treasure," he said. "Take care of Jim and shout if you need help."

When the doctor had gone the pirates set off to look for the treasure. They were all heavily armed and carried picks and shovels.

The chart said the treasure was buried beneath a tall tree on Mizzenmast Hill. As the pirates climbed the hill they argued about which tree it could be.

The pirates stared at it in silence. Then they heard a strange, high voice: "Fifteen men on the dead man's chest," it sang.

The pirates were terrified. "It's Flint's ghost," they gasped "It's only someone trying to scare us," Long John said calmly.

Suddenly one of the pirates yelled. The others ran over to him. There, at the foot of a tree, lay a human skeleton which was pointing towards the top of the hill.

The pirates struggled on up the hill. At last they saw a tall tree in front of them. They charged towards it, then stopped in their tracks.

A huge hole had been dug at the foot of the tree. Some one had got there before the pirates and all of the treasure had gone.

Long John secretly gave Jim a pistol. "Stand by for trouble," he whispered. "He is always changing sides," thought Jim.

The pirates jumped into the hole and began digging. One of them held up a coin. "Did we come all this way just for this?" he roared.

He climbed out of the hole. "Down with Long John," he cried. Suddenly shots rang out from the bushes and two of the pirates dropped dead.

The next minute Dr. Livesey and Ben Gunn rushed into the clearing, their guns smoking. The three pirates still alive ran away.

"Quick," cried the doctor. "We must head them off before they reach the boats." They charged down the hill with Long John hobbling

along behind them. They reached the beach before the pirates, knocked a hole in one boat and pushed out to sea in the other.

As they rowed to the ship, Dr. Livesey told Jim that when Ben Gunn was alone on the island he had found the treasure. He had dug it up and taken it to his cave.

"When I saw the ship had gone," said Dr. Livesey, "I led our friends to Ben's cave. I heard Silver's plans to find the treasure and came to rescue you."

They left one man on board the ship to guard it, then headed for Ben's cave. It was enormous. Great heaps of coins and gold bars glinted in the firelight.

The squire and captain were very pleased to see Jim safe. That night they and the loyal sailors had a huge feast to celebrate finding Captain Flint's treasure.

Next day they loaded the treasure on to the ship. Then they sailed away with Ben and Long John, leaving the three pirates on the island. Soon they reached South America and hired a new crew. Here Long John escaped with a sack of gold. He knew he would be hanged for piracy if he went back to England. The squire and the doctor sailed home and gave Jim some of the gold. He never forgot his adventure on Treasure Island.

Treasure Island was written by Robert Louis Stevenson. It first appeared in a children's magazine, called *Young Folks,* and was then published as a book in 1883. It has since become a children's classic.

Treasure Island is an exciting story about bloodthirsty buccaneers. The novel follows the adventures of a brave boy called Jim Hawkins, who time and time again outwits cunning Long John Silver and his band of ruthless pirates in the search for buried gold.

Robert Louis Stevenson (1850-1894) was born in Edinburgh and studied both engineering and law before taking up writing. He wrote many essays, stories and descriptions of his travels, such as *Travels with a Donkey. Treasure Island* was his first novel and this was followed by other adventure stories, such as *Kidnapped* and *The Master of Ballantrae.*

GULLIVER'S TRAVELS
IN LILLIPUT

JONATHAN SWIFT

Many years ago there lived in England a man called Lemuel Gulliver. He loved travelling and had already sailed all round the world.

One day he boarded a ship bound for the Far East, little knowing that this was to be the strangest adventure of his life.

The voyage began well, but as the ship approached the East Indies a mighty storm blew the ship a long way off course.

Soon there was no fresh food or water left and some of the sailors caught a fever. Gulliver tried to look after them but many men died.

One night there was another fierce storm. Strong winds and rough seas drove the ship on to sharp rocks and wrecked it.

Gulliver swam for his life, hoping there was land nearby. At last, just as he was giving up hope, he felt ground beneath his feet.

He stumbled ashore and fell down on a grassy slope. The grass was short and very soft and he was so tired, he was soon fast asleep.

Some of the crew tried to escape in a rowing boat, but it overturned in the huge waves and everyone drowned except for Gulliver.

When Gulliver finally awoke after a long, deep sleep, he tried to stand up. To his surprise, he found that he could not move.

His arms and legs were tied to the ground and his hair was pinned down. He could not even turn his head away from the glare of the sun.

Suddenly Gulliver felt some thing small and light move up his body and stop just below his chin. He peered downwards as best he could.

To his astonishment he saw a tiny man, only about six inches tall, standing on his chest and pointing a bow and arrow at his nose.

Then about forty more little men scrambled up on to Gulliver's chest. None of them was bigger than his hand and they were all armed.

Gulliver was so surprised, he shouted loudly. The noise was deafening to the little men and they all fell over or ran away in fright.

But soon their courage returned and they came back again. One brave man crept right up to Gulliver's face. "Hekina degul!" he cried in a shrill voice, staring at Gulliver in amazement.

68

Gulliver struggled to get free. He managed to break some of the strings tying him and to free one arm. Then he pulled out the pegs holding down his hair so he could turn his head.

But when he tried to sit up hundreds of tiny men all round him shouted and fired arrows at him. These pricked Gulliver's face and hands painfully, like thousands of tiny needles.

Other men jabbed at Gulliver's sides with spears but luckily the spears did not pierce his leather jerkin. "I had better lie still and see what happens," thought Gulliver.

After a while the men stopped firing arrows and Gulliver heard a knocking sound. He turned his head to see what was happening.

The little men were building a platform near him. It was eighteen inches high and big enough to hold four of the tiny people.

An important looking man went up on to the platform and made a long speech in a strange language. Gulliver did not understand a word.

He spoke back and tried to show that he was hungry by putting a finger to his mouth. He had not eaten since before the shipwreck.

The man understood. He shouted orders and the tiny people propped ladders against Gulliver. They climbed up them and walked towards Gulliver's mouth, carrying baskets of food.

Then Gulliver showed them he was thirsty and they brought him barrels and barrels of wine. He drank each barrel in one swig.

The people were so delighted by this that they danced on Gulliver's chest. He was surprised they were no longer frightened of him.

In the baskets there were small joints of meat, and loaves of bread the size of buttons. Gulliver ate two of everything at a time. The tiny people were amazed at how much he could eat.

When he had finished his meal a nobleman from the Court walked up to his face and waved a message at him. It was from the Emperor.

He made a speech and then left. Gulliver soon fell into a deep sleep. He did not know there had been a sleeping drug in his wine.

While Gulliver slept, five hundred carpenters built a giant trolley next to him, hoisted him on to it and harnessed it to 1,500 horses.

They set off towards Mildendo, the capital city of the land. The emperor had ordered that Gulliver be taken there.

The journey took over a day and the procession finally stopped in front of a grand temple not far from the city. The temple was to be

Gulliver's home, as it was the largest building in the land. It was just big enough for Gulliver to lie down in.

The emperor came to look at Gulliver. He watched from the top of a nearby tower as Gulliver was chained to the temple.

Once Gulliver's chains were secure, his ropes were cut and he could stand up. The crowd gasped in wonder as he rose to his feet.

Towering above the crowds, Gulliver had a bird's eye view of the countryside around him. Everything was tiny. "It looks like a miniature garden," thought Gulliver. The tallest trees were only about three feet high and the fields seemed no larger than people's flowerbeds in England. The city not far away looked like a brightly coloured model village.

73

The emperor came down from the tower and ordered his servants to give Gulliver more food and drink that was ready for him. It was piled into little carts and the servants pushed them forwards to a place where Gulliver could bend down and reach them easily.

He picked up one cart and emptied it in two gulps, then he picked up another. Altogether he ate twenty whole cartloads of food.

When Gulliver had finished eating, the emperor went forwards to talk to him. He held his sword drawn, in case Gulliver attacked him.

Gulliver lay on his side so he and the emperor could talk to each other, but neither of them understood a word the other was saying.

Gulliver tried many languages, but the emperor did not understand any of them. He went away, leaving guards to protect Gulliver.

Everyone wanted to see the giant man. They pushed closer and closer and some men dodged past the guards and fired arrows at Gulliver.

The guards seized six of the ruffians and pushed them towards Gulliver to be punished. The men struggled and howled with fright.

Gulliver picked them up. He put five in his pocket and lifted the sixth to his mouth, as if he were about to eat him alive. The little man screamed and screamed, especially when Gulliver took out his penknife. But Gulliver just cut the ropes round his hands and gently put him down on the ground. He did the same with the rest of the ruffians and they all ran away.

As the days passed, thousands of people flocked to look at Gulliver. So many people went to see him that the emperor was worried no work was being done. He ordered that no one was allowed to visit Gulliver a second time unless they paid a lot of money.

He held meetings with his nobles to decide what to do with Gulliver. They thought he might be dangerous and that they ought to kill him.

Then two of Gulliver's guards went to one of the meetings and told how kind he had been to the rough people in the crowd.

This pleased the emperor and he ordered all the villages around Mildendo to supply enough food for Gulliver every day.

Then he gave Gulliver six hundred servants of his own. They lived in tents on either side of the entrance to Gulliver's temple home.

Gulliver learnt the new language quickly and within three weeks he was able to talk to the emperor. "Please set me free," he begged. "You must wait for a while," the emperor replied. From then on Gulliver went to him every day and asked him again.

Three hundred tailors measured Gulliver for clothes and six clever men were sent to teach him their strange language.

Then one day the emperor sent two officers to search Gulliver for dangerous weapons. They wanted to look in Gulliver's pockets, so he picked them up and put them into each of his pockets in turn. The officers made a long list of everything they found.

When they had finished their search, the two officers went to the emperor and read their list out loud to him.

"In the Man Mountain's right coat pocket we found a sheet of cloth big enough to be a carpet." This was Gulliver's handkerchief.

"In the left pocket there was a silver chest full of strange powder which made us sneeze." This was Gulliver's snuff box.

"In another pocket were sheets of paper bound together. They were covered with black marks which must have been writing."

"In a waistcoat pocket was a thing with poles sticking out from it. We think that the Man Mountain combs his head with this machine."

"In another pocket was an iron tube longer than a man. It had a wooden handle and bits of iron on it. We have no idea what this was."

78

"In one of the top pockets there was a round thing on a chain. It made a ticking noise and the Man Mountain kept looking at it."

"In another pocket he had a net full of gold coins. He said this was his purse. This was all we found in the Man Mountain's pockets."

When he had heard the list the emperor ordered his troops to surround Gulliver and told him to draw his scimitar. Gulliver waved it in the air and everyone gasped in fear.

Next he had to pull out the strange iron tube. Gulliver fired his pistol into the air and hundreds of soldiers fell down with fright. Then Gulliver handed his weapons to the emperor's guards.

As time went by Gulliver learnt that the island he was on was called Lilliput. He tried to please its tiny people, hoping one day they would free him. They soon grew to trust him. Even the children were not scared of him and played hide and seek in his hair.

One day Gulliver watched a strange competition. The men of Lilliput did tricks on a tightrope to win posts at the emperor's court.

Whoever was best won the best job. Flimnap had won his job as treasurer by making the rope higher and doing double somersaults.

There was another competition, called Leaping and Creeping. The emperor and one of his ministers held out a stick and the competitors had to leap over it or creep under it. The best people won coloured ribbons to tie round their waists.

One day Gulliver decided he would entertain the emperor. He made a platform out of a handkerchief tied tightly over some sticks.

He lifted some of the emperor's cavalry on to the platform and they staged a mock battle. The emperor was delighted with the show.

He persuaded the empress to let Gulliver hold her level with the platform so that she could have a good view of the performance.

During the show a messenger arrived. He told the emperor that some shepherds had found a large, strange object in a field.

He described the object and Gulliver realised that it was his hat, which he had lost. The next day the shepherds brought it to him.

It was very dusty because it had been dragged along the ground all the way to the city, but Gulliver was pleased to have it back.

81

Gulliver wanted to visit the palace, but the gate was too small for him to go through and the walls too high for him to step over.

Then he had an idea. He went to the Royal Park and cut down some trees with his penknife. With the wood from these he made two stools.

At last the emperor set Gulliver free. He could go where he liked as long as he asked permission and stayed on the main roads. The emperor told him he could go into the city.

Everyone was warned Gulliver was coming. They stayed indoors so they would not be trodden on and watched from their windows as Gulliver stepped carefully through the streets.

He lay down and looked through the windows of the palace into the royal apartments. The windows had been left open for him.

It was like looking into a doll's house. The rooms were furnished with tiny tables and chairs to fit the tiny people who used them.

He took them back to the palace and put one on each side of the wall. Then he used them as stepping stones to climb over the wall.

The empress was sitting by one of the palace windows with her children. They were all waiting to see the Man Mountain.

The empress smiled when she saw Gulliver. "Welcome," she said and she held out her hand so that Gulliver could kiss it.

One morning, soon after Gulliver's visit to the palace, Reldresaal, the emperor's secretary, paid him a visit.

"There are problems at court," he told Gulliver. "There are two rival groups of men trying to win power in the land."

"One group, the Tramecksans, wears high heels and the other, the Slamecksans, low heels. Neither group will speak to the other."

"The emperor likes low heels, so at the moment the Slamecksans have more power. But a civil war could break out at any time."

"As well as these problems," Reldresaal went on, "we are at war with a neighbouring island called Blefescu where the people are no bigger than us. You might think the war rather strange. We are fighting over which is the right end to start eating a boiled egg.

84

We always used to break our eggs at the big end, but many years ago one of the princes cut his finger as he broke open his egg.

His father, the emperor of Lilliput, at once ordered that from then on everyone had to break open their eggs at the smaller end.

But many people refused to do this. Thousands preferred to die rather than give in to the new law and break their eggs at the small end.

The people of Blefescu still broke their eggs at the big end, so many of the rebels from Lilliput fled to Blefescu and lived there.

The two kingdoms have been at war for years and many people have been killed. Now Blefescu's fleet is preparing to invade us."

"The emperor needs your help if he is to win this war," said Reldresaal. "I will do what I can," Gulliver promised him.

Gulliver decided to look at Blefescu. He walked to the coast of Lilliput and lay down behind a small hill to spy on the other island.

He took out his telescope so he could study the enemy fleet more closely. There were about fifty warships and some smaller ones.

Gulliver returned home and asked for ropes and iron bars. He twisted the ropes together to make them strong and bent the bars into hooks.

Then he went back to the coast and waded into the sea, carrying the ropes and hooks. He headed towards Blefescu's fleet.

Gulliver had to swim across the middle part of the channel between Lilliput and Blefescu, as the sea was deep. As only his head was

above water, the enemy did not see him until he was very close. They screamed with fright and jumped overboard to escape.

Gulliver fastened ropes to the ships and cut their anchors loose. The people of Blefescu fired thousands of arrows at him.

Gulliver put on his glasses so he could carry on with his work. The tiny arrows stuck in his face and hands but his eyes were safe.

He tied all the ropes together and headed back for Lilliput, pulling the ships behind him. The enemy shouted with rage when they saw their entire fleet being towed away.

As Gulliver approached the shore of Lilliput he saw the emperor and the court waiting for him. "Long live the emperor!" he cried and everyone welcomed him home with shouts and cheers.

The emperor was not satisfied for long with Gulliver capturing the fleet. "You must help me conquer Blefescu," he told him.

"I won't make free people into slaves," said Gulliver. The emperor was annoyed. After this he was no longer very friendly to Gulliver.

Three weeks later six ambassadors came from Blefescu to make peace with Lilliput. Gulliver met them while they were there and

they invited him to visit Blefescu later on. The emperor of Lilliput gave him permission to go, but he looked very angry.

A few days after the ambassadors had left Gulliver was able to do the emperor a service. Late one night he was woken up by shouting outside his temple.

"Come quickly," a voice cried. "The empress's palace is on fire." Gulliver ran to the palace, trying not to step on the tiny people rushing around everywhere.

There was chaos at the palace. The little people were passing buckets of water along to the fire, but the buckets were only the size of thimbles and

the flames roared as fiercely as ever. Gulliver helped and within minutes he had put out the fire. The palace was saved and he went back home to bed.

89

Gulliver was happy living in Lilliput and had every thing he needed. Two hundred needlewomen made shirts for him.

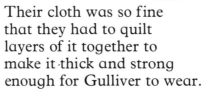

Their cloth was so fine that they had to quilt layers of it together to make it thick and strong enough for Gulliver to wear.

To find out Gulliver's size, the women measured round his thumb. They said they could work out the rest of his measurements from this.

Three hundred tailors made a new suit for Gulliver. They measured him by dropping a plumb line from his neck to the ground.

When Gulliver's suit was finished, it fitted well, but it looked as if it was made of patchwork all the same colour.

The emperor was curious to see how Gulliver lived. One evening he and his family went to have dinner with Gulliver at his home.

Gulliver picked them up and put them on the table in front of him. They had a magnificent feast and enjoyed themselves.

Three hundred chefs cooked Gulliver's food every day and 120 waiters served it to him, hoisting it on to the table with pulleys.

Flimnap, the treasurer, was also there. He did not like Gulliver and kept glaring at him, but Gulliver took no notice and went on eating.

Flimnap was annoyed and whispered to the emperor, complaining about how much it cost to feed Gulliver. The emperor looked cross.

Late one night, as Gulliver was planning his visit to Blefescu, he had a surprise visit from one of the highest nobles of the court.

He told Gulliver to send his servants away, then spoke to him secretly. "Your life is in great danger," he said.

"You have enemies at court. Flimnap and the admiral have accused you of being a traitor and have written out a list of your crimes."

They say you have been plotting against the emperor with the people of Blefescu and that you should be punished by death.

Flimnap suggested that your temple be set on fire and that you be shot with poisoned arrows as you try to escape from the blaze.

But Reldresaal reminded the court of how useful you had been. He suggested it might be kinder to spare your life and just make you blind.

The emperor agreed to this but thought you should also be slowly starved, to save money. The court praised him for his great generosity."

Gulliver knew he had to act quickly. He wrote to the emperor, saying he was leaving at once for his promised visit to Blefescu.

He did not wait for an answer to his letter but set off straightaway for the coast. He stole one of the largest ships in the Lilliputian fleet and tied a rope to its prow.

He took off his clothes, bundled them up and put them on the ship. Then, pulling the ship along behind him, he waded out to sea and swam across the channel to Blefescu.

When Gulliver reached Blefescu, he went to the capital city. The king came out to meet him and Gulliver lay down to kiss his hand. The king was not at all scared and welcomed Gulliver warmly, saying he could stay in Blefescu for as long as he liked.

A few days later Gulliver saw something odd out at sea. It was a full-sized boat which had overturned! Gulliver was very excited.

He rushed back to the king. "Please help me to get this boat," he begged him. "It may be my only chance to return home."

The king lent him twenty big ships and three thousand sailors. They sailed round the island to the boat and Gulliver swam out to it.

He tied the boat to the ships and the sailors towed it slowly back to the shore while Gulliver swam behind it, pushing it along.

When they reached the shore Gulliver pulled the boat on to the beach. With the help of the king's men he got it ready for the voyage home.

Five hundred men made sails for the boat. They quilted together thirteen layers of the strongest material in the kingdom.

Gulliver cut down some tall trees to make a mast and oars and he found a heavy stone to use as an anchor. The boat was soon finished.

He decided to take some tiny cows and sheep home with him. He would have liked to take people as well but the king would not allow it.

At last everything was ready. The king was sad that Gulliver was going and gave him fifty bags of gold coins and a picture of himself as

a leaving present. Gulliver put the picture in one of his gloves to keep it safe, then he kissed the king's hand and set sail for home.

95

Gulliver had only been at sea a few days when, to his excitement, he saw a ship. It was an English ship. Gulliver called and waved.

Luckily the sailors saw him and steered towards the boat. Soon Gulliver was aboard with his tiny animals, feeling very relieved.

Gulliver's Travels was written by Jonathan Swift and first published in 1726. It was an instant success with both children and adults and has remained a classic ever since.

In this book, the first part of *Gulliver's Travels* is retold. This is the story of Gulliver's extraordinary adventures in Lilliput, where the people are only six inches tall. We see how Gulliver wins the trust of the Lilliputians and adapts to life on their island. Swift shows with great wit how ridiculous people's customs and attitudes can be.

Jonathan Swift (1667-1745) grew up in Ireland. He worked as a secretary to a politician, then became a priest. He was involved in politics throughout his career and wrote many treatises on politics and religion. *Gulliver's Travels*, a satire on the political life of the times, was his most famous book.

"Welcome," said the captain. "Where have you come from?" Gulliver told him about his adventures on Lilliput and showed him the tiny animals.

The captain was amazed. Gulliver promised him some animals and gold for his voyage home, and they sailed safely back to England.

THE ADVENTURES OF
KING ARTHUR

The Sword in the Stone

Long, long ago, in Britain, when the world was still full of magic, there was a wise old wizard called Merlin. He could see into the future and work magic spells.

One wild and stormy winter's night Merlin was staying in a castle. It was the stronghold of his friend, King Uther. The Queen had just given birth to Uther's first and only son.

The King told Merlin he feared a plot to kill his son and that he had a plan to keep him safe.

Just before midnight, Merlin opened a small, secret door and slipped out of the castle.

Under his cloak he was carrying a bundle, and in the bundle was the baby boy.

The years passed and Uther died. No one knew he had a son to inherit his crown, so his knights fought each other to win the kingdom.

Far away in the Welsh hills, Merlin heard of these fights for the crown. As only he knew that Uther had a son, he set off at once for London.

There Merlin said to the archbishop, "The time has come to find the new king. You must call all the knights in the land to London."

The archbishop summoned all the knights to come on Christmas Day. Hundreds came and they crowded into the Abbey to pray. After the service, as they were leaving, they stopped in amazement.

A huge block of stone had appeared in the churchyard and in it was a sword. Round the stone were carved the words: WHOEVER PULLS THIS SWORD OUT OF THIS STONE IS THE TRUE BORN KING OF BRITAIN.

Eagerly the knights leapt on to the stone and one after another they struggled to pull out the sword. Even the strongest knights could not move it an inch. "The king is not here," said the archbishop.

"Send messengers round the kingdom," he ordered. "Tell every knight what is written on the stone. On New Year's Day we shall hold a tournament. Perhaps the king will be amongst those who come to joust."

Knights, with their squires, families and servants, rode to London from all over the land. They set up their tents on the field and practised for the tournament.

On New Year's Day the knights went to the Abbey churchyard. Each one tried to pull the sword out of the stone, but struggle as they might, no one could move it.

Among the knights who came to London for the tournament were Sir Ector and his two sons, Kay and Arthur. Kay had just been knighted but Arthur was only sixteen and was too young to be a knight.

On the way to the tournament Sir Kay suddenly found he had forgotten his sword. "I must have left it at the inn," he said. "I will fetch it for you," said Arthur and set off at a gallop for the town.

When he reached the inn, the door was locked. Arthur knocked but everyone had gone to the tournament. "I must find a sword," he thought. "This is Kay's first joust and he cannot fight without one."

He rode away, wondering what to do. Passing the Abbey churchyard, he saw the sword in the stone. Without reading the words on the stone, he leapt off his horse, ran to the stone and pulled out the sword.

Arthur galloped back to the tournament. "Here's a sword," he said, handing it to Kay. Kay stared at it for a moment, then looked at Arthur. He knew where the sword came from and snatched it.

He hurried to Sir Ector. "Look, father," he shouted. "Here is the sword from the stone. I must be the King of Britain." But Sir Ector knew his son well. "Let us go back to the churchyard," he said quietly.

In the Abbey, Sir Ector made his elder son swear on The Bible to tell the truth about the sword. Kay bowed his head and said, "Arthur gave it to me." Then Arthur told Sir Ector what he had done.

They went into the churchyard and Arthur put the sword back into the stone. Sir Ector seized it but it would not move. Then Kay tried but it still would not move. "It is your turn, Arthur," said Sir Ector.

Arthur gripped the sword, pulled and it slid easily out of the stone. Sir Ector and Kay knelt down at once. Arthur looked at them in surprise. "What is the matter? Why are you kneeling?" he asked.

"Read the words on the stone," said Sir Ector. "I am not your real father," he explained. "When you were a baby, Merlin brought you to me so that you would be safe from Uther's enemies."

"Now we must tell the Archbishop that we have found the King." But the other knights would not believe it. They went back to their homes, agreeing to meet again in London to settle the matter.

They met at Whitsun and crowds watched the knights try their luck. Only Arthur could pull out the sword. The crowds shouted, "Arthur is King!" And knights and people knelt to swear their loyalty.

The Lady of the Lake

So Arthur was crowned King and set up his court at Camelot. He gathered Merlin and all the best knights round him, and brought peace to the land. Anyone in trouble could go to his court for help.

One day a young man came to the court, leading a horse carrying a dead knight. The man told Arthur that his master had been killed by a knight in the forest who swore to kill every knight who passed.

"I seek revenge!" cried the man. "The knight, Sir Pellinore, challenged my good master, then fought and killed him. Is there any knight here who will punish him for my master's death?"

"Let me go," a young man called Grifflet begged the King. Arthur agreed and knighted him at once. Grifflet set off, but that night his horse came back to Camelot. Grifflet was badly wounded.

The next day Arthur rode into the forest. He was very angry that Grifflet had been so badly hurt. And he wanted to fight Sir Pellinore himself, in revenge for his knight's death.

Riding through the forest, he came to a clearing and saw three robbers attacking Merlin. Arthur charged at them and they ran into the trees. "Merlin, why didn't your magic powers save you?" asked Arthur.

"I did not use them," said Merlin. "But you are in far greater danger than I was. Sir Pellinore is one of the strongest knights in the world. Turn back." But Arthur rode on, so Merlin went with him.

Soon they saw Sir Pellinore's tent through the trees. Suddenly a mighty knight on a huge horse appeared in front of them. "I am Sir Pellinore!" he shouted. "If you come any further, I will kill you."

"We shall fight to the death," cried Arthur. He and Pellinore rode to opposite ends of a clearing, then they levelled their lances and thundered towards each other.

Each lance clashed so hard on the shields that they snapped. A squire brought new ones and they charged again. This time Arthur was thrown from his horse.

Arthur leapt to his feet. "How good are you with a sword?" he shouted. Pellinore jumped down from his horse and they fought on.

Arthur fought bravely but Pellinore was stronger. They hacked and slashed, then Pellinore gave Arthur's sword such a blow it broke.

"Now you are in my power," cried Pellinore. "Surrender or die." But Arthur rushed at him, threw him down and they wrestled on the ground.

Soon Pellinore had Arthur at his mercy again. He was about to cut off his head when Merlin cried, "Stop! You must not kill the King."

Pellinore looked at Merlin in surprise. "I must kill him," he said. "If he lives, he will never forgive me. My life and honour depend on it."

Merlin secretly cast a spell on Pellinore, who slumped to the ground. "A brave knight," said Merlin, "asleep he will do no harm."

Arthur lay on the grass, badly wounded. Merlin helped him on to his horse and led him through the forest to the home of a hermit. The old man dressed Arthur's wounds and gave him medicines to drink.

After a few days, Arthur was well enough to leave. "Merlin," he said, "what shall I do? I have no sword." Merlin smiled and said, "We shall go to the Lake of Avalon. There we shall find a sword for you."

Next morning, they set off and rode for many days until they came to a misty lake in the hills. On the bank, Arthur stopped his horse and stared in surprise. "Look, Merlin," he whispered.

Rising out of the lake was a hand, holding a magnificent, jewelled sword and scabbard.

Walking across the water towards them was a beautiful lady. "It is the Lady of the Lake," said Merlin quietly. "She lives in a magic castle under the water. You must ask her for the sword and scabbard."

They got off their horses, tied them to a tree and waited on the bank for the Lady.

When she came up to Arthur, he bowed and took her hand. "My Lady," he said, "I beg you to give me the sword." "It is called Excalibur," she said. "You may take it." She pointed to a boat hidden in the reeds.

Arthur stepped into the boat and, as if by magic, it floated across the water to the hand. Arthur grasped the sword and scabbard and at once the hand slid silently beneath the water and was gone.

When the boat brought Arthur back to the shore, the Lady had vanished. Joyfully he showed the sword and scabbard to Merlin. "Which do you like best?" asked Merlin. "The sword," said Arthur. Merlin frowned.

"You will win many battles with the sword," he said, "but the scabbard is worth more. While wearing it, you will not bleed, even badly wounded. Let us go," and they rode back to a great welcome at Camelot.

The Knights of the Round Table

The years passed and Arthur fell in love with the beautiful Lady Guinevere. "Merlin," he said one day, "I wish to marry Guinevere." "You will not always be happy together," Merlin warned him.

Arthur would not change his mind, so Merlin went to Guinevere's father, Sir Leo. "The King loves your beautiful daughter and wishes to marry her," he said. Sir Leo was delighted and gave his consent at once.

The marriage was to be at Easter and a few days before, Guinevere came to Camelot with many knights. Then she was married to Arthur and crowned Queen.

After the ceremony, Arthur led Guinevere to the great hall. A magnificent feast was laid out on a huge round table which Sir Leo had given Arthur as a wedding present.

Before the feast began, Arthur stood up and spoke to his knights. "From this great day you shall be known as the Knights of the Round Table," he said.

"Each knight must swear to be noble and brave, to fight for just causes and to always help the weak and those in distress. We shall meet once a year at Camelot to tell of our adventures and the Knights of the Round Table shall become famous throughout the land."

The Knights stood up and each one swore a solemn oath to follow these rules.

The Plot to kill Arthur

King Arthur had a wicked sister, Morgan le Fay, who was married to Lord Uriens. She hated Arthur and had fallen in love with a handsome knight, Sir Accolon.

Morgan decided to kill both Arthur and her husband, so that she could marry Accolon and rule Arthur's kingdom with him.

Accolon loved Morgan and would do anything she asked. He did not know she was wicked and knew evil spells.

One day Arthur and Accolon went hunting stags in the forest. By evening they were lost. Trying to find their way home, they came to a lake.

Floating by the shore was a strange, beautiful boat, lit by torches. Lovely maidens on the deck invited the tired men to eat and rest.

A splendid feast was spread out for them. They ate and then fell asleep, not knowing they were under the spell of Morgan le Fay.

When Arthur woke, he was chained in a dark prison with twenty knights. They told him they were the prisoners of a knight called Sir Damas.

Soon a maid came into the prison. "Sir Damas will set you free," she told them "if one of you will fight and kill an enemy knight for him."

"I will fight," cried Arthur. So the maid unlocked his chains and led him out of the prison. She gave him armour, a helmet and a sword. "Here is Excalibur," she said, "sent to you by your sister Morgan."

When Accolon woke, a dwarf offered him a sword. "Queen Morgan sends you this and begs you to fight an unknown knight for her," he said. Accolon took it and went to the battlefield where Arthur was waiting.

The two knights met with their visors down so they could not recognize each other. The battle began and Arthur fought fiercely but his sword was useless. Again and again he was wounded. Then his sword snapped.

Accolon raised his sword to kill Arthur. But, at that moment, the Lady of the Lake appeared, casting a spell on Accolon who dropped it. Arthur saw it was the real Excalibur, seized it and cried, "Now die!"

Arthur struck Accolon so hard, he fell down, blood gushing from his head. "Kill me, noble knight," said Accolon. "You have won." Arthur lowered his sword when he heard Accolon's voice and knelt at his side.

"Who are you?" he asked. "Accolon," the knight whispered. Arthur raised his visor and Accolon wept when he saw who it was. He told Arthur that he had been sent by Morgan to kill him and begged forgiveness.

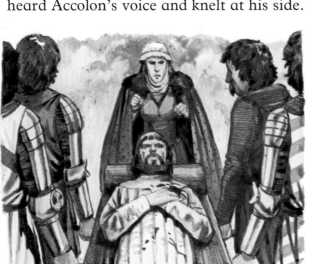

Then Accolon died from his wounds and Arthur swore revenge on Morgan. He sent Accolon's body to her. She was heartbroken when she saw Accolon and furious that Arthur had Excalibur again.

Determined to steal Excalibur, she rode to the abbey where Arthur was recovering from his wounds and asked to see him. "He is asleep," said a nun. "Do not wake him," said Morgan. "I will sit at his bedside."

She crept quietly into the room where Arthur lay sleeping, hoping to steal the sword. But Arthur slept with it clasped in his hand and Morgan did not dare touch it in case he woke up and saw her.

Then she saw the magic scabbard lying on the bed. "At least I can take that," she thought. Looking round to make sure no one was watching, she hid it under her cloak, quickly left the abbey and rode away.

When Arthur woke up and found the scabbard gone, he called the nuns. He leapt up when he heard Morgan had been to the abbey. "Saddle my horse," he cried. "I will go after her. She must not escape."

Morgan soon heard Arthur and a knight galloping after her. "He shall not have the scabbard," she screamed and threw it into a lake. Then she used her magic to turn herself and her servant into huge rocks.

Arthur did not see the scabbard fall into the lake and rode past the rocks, searching everywhere for Morgan. He could not understand how she had vanished and angrily turned back towards Camelot.

That evening, a servant girl came to the court. "Queen Morgan sent me,' she said to Arthur. "She begs you to forgive her and offers you this jewelled cloak as a token of her love for you."

Arthur suspected it might be a trick. "You put it on first," he told the girl. "Oh no, Sir," she said, afraid. "Put it on," ordered Arthur. Slowly she did so and in a flash the cloak burst into flames.

Once again, Morgan le Fay's plot to kill King Arthur had failed. Angrily he banished her from Camelot for ever.

Sir Lancelot's Adventure

At King Arthur's court was a knight called Sir Lancelot. Strong, very brave and handsome, he won more tournaments, fought more battles and set out on more dangerous quests than any other knight.

Although he was King Arthur's most trusted knight, Sir Lancelot had fallen in love with Arthur's queen, Guinevere. Lancelot knew he could never marry her but had sworn to love and protect her always.

One morning Lancelot rode off in search of adventure with his cousin, Sir Lionel. By the afternoon, the knights were hot and tired in their armour. "Let's rest under this tree for a while," said Lancelot.

After tying up their horses, Lancelot lay on the cool grass and went to sleep. Lionel was leaning sleepily against the tree when he heard horses' hoofs. Then he saw a huge knight chasing three others across the plain.

117

The huge knight attacked the three other knights and soon defeated them. He tied them to their horses, then led the horses away.

Without waking Lancelot, Lionel leapt on to his horse and rode up to him. But the huge knight only laughed when Lionel challenged him.

Then he charged. Lionel fought hard but the knight was too strong. He tied up Lionel and led him away to a castle with the other captives.

Lancelot was still asleep and did not know what had happened. While he slept, four ladies rode by and stopped to look at him. "How handsome he is," they sighed. Each one wished he would fall in love with her.

One of the ladies was Morgan le Fay. "I have a plan," she said. "I will cast a spell on him so that we can take him, still asleep, to my castle. When he wakes, I will tell him to choose one of us as his love, or die."

When Lancelot woke from his enchanted sleep, he was in a dark dungeon. He did not know where he was or how he got there. He tried to find a way out but the door was locked and the windows barred. Then

the four ladies came in and ordered him to choose one of them as his love. "I can love no one but my Lady Guinevere," said Lancelot. Morgan le Fay threatened him with death but he would not give in.

Lancelot was left alone in his prison. That night the maid who brought his supper said, "Sir, I will help you escape if you will fight a battle for my father, who is a noble knight." Lancelot agreed at once.

Early next morning, the maid set Lancelot free and gave him armour and a horse. Then he fought the battle, winning easily. After saying goodbye to the maid and her father, he set off to look for Sir Lionel.

After many days, Lancelot met a maiden and told her of his search. "A wicked knight, Sir Tarquin, lives in a castle near here. He has captured many knights. Perhaps Sir Lionel is in his prison," she said.

She led Lancelot to the castle and, as they approached it, they saw Sir Tarquin, leading a captured Knight of the Round Table. Lancelot put on his helmet. "Defend yourself, Sir," he shouted.

Lancelot and Sir Tarquin charged each other so violently that their horses both fell under them. The two knights were thrown to the ground and they lay there for a while, stunned and unable to move.

Then they staggered to their feet and fought on with their swords. They struck blow after blow, wounding each other many times, but neither could win. After many hours they were too tired to fight.

"You are the bravest knight I have met," said Tarquin, "Let us fight no more." "Agreed," said Lancelot, "but first promise to free your captives." "I will if you tell me your name," said Tarquin.

When Lancelot told him, Tarquin cried out, "Then we fight on. Long ago I swore to kill you in revenge for the death of my brother." They fought on until Lancelot struck Tarquin so hard he died instantly.

Lancelot took Tarquin's keys and went to his castle. There he found Lionel and many other Knights of the Round Table locked in the dungeon. "You are free," he cried. "Come, let us all return to Camelot."

Lancelot and Guinevere

As the years passed, Arthur and his knights rode out on many quests, fought battles and won great victories. These conquests brought peace to the Kingdom.

Although they always fought bravely, some knights were killed or died of their wounds, and there were empty seats at the great Round Table.

New knights came to Camelot but some were not true to the oath they swore and plotted against their King.

The leader of these knights was Arthur's nephew, Mordred. He wanted to destroy the brotherhood of the Round Table and become king. So he plotted to cause trouble between Arthur and Lancelot.

Sir Lancelot still loved Guinevere but was loyal to his King. He knew that Mordred was spreading lies about him to make Arthur jealous, so he met Guinevere in secret. But Mordred's spies were watching.

Mordred went to Arthur. "Lancelot and Queen Guinevere are traitors to the king," he said. "The punishment is death. They must die." But Arthur would not believe him. "I must have proof," he said angrily.

That evening, Lancelot went to Guinevere's room. Suddenly there was a shout outside the door, "Arrest the traitors!" It was Mordred and his men. Seizing his sword, Lancelot fought his way out and escaped.

Mordred went at once to Arthur. "I have proof of their treachery," he said. Sadly, Arthur agreed to fight Lancelot. "But what about the Queen?" asked Mordred. "Traitors should die at the stake."

One grey morning, Guinevere was led out and tied to the stake. But just as the fire was lit, Lancelot and his men charged up. He cut Guinevere free and carried her away on his horse to his castle in Wales.

123

The Traitor Mordred

Although Arthur was secretly happy that Guinevere's life had been saved, he knew he must still fight Lancelot. Assembling his men, he set off for Wales but some knights sided with Lancelot against him.

There were many fierce battles but neither side won. Sad to see so many brave knights killed, Lancelot took Guinevere back to Arthur and then sailed to France.

The war should have ended then but Gawain, a Knight of the Round Table, hated Lancelot for accidentally killing his brother. Gawain persuaded Arthur to go to France to fight Lancelot there.

Before he sailed, Arthur sent for Mordred, and told him to rule the Kingdom until he came back again with his knights.

This was the chance Mordred had been waiting for. After a few weeks he spread the news that the King was dead. Mordred crowned himself King and said that he would marry Guinevere.

When Guinevere heard this, she fled to London and sent a messenger to Arthur, telling him of Mordred's treachery.

Arthur at once sailed back to England. When he reached the harbour at Dover, Mordred and his army were waiting for him. There was a terrible battle but Arthur won and Mordred retreated.

Gawain was badly wounded. Arthur knelt at his side. "I caused this trouble," Gawain said. "Forgive me and forgive Sir Lancelot. Your enemies would not dare fight you if he were here." Then he died.

The Last Battle

Arthur wept for Gawain; then marched off to fight Mordred again. When their armies met, there was a dreadful battle. At the end, only four men were still standing; Arthur, two of his knights and Mordred.

Arthur looked in despair at the dying and dead knights. Then, seeing Mordred still alive, he shouted, "Traitor!" and ran him through with a spear. As he died, Mordred struck Arthur a huge blow on his head.

The two knights saw Arthur fall and ran to him. Gently they carried him to a small chapel near a lake, where they could tend his wounds. Raising his head, Arthur looked round him and recognized the lake.

He handed his sword to Sir Bedivere, one of the knights. "Take Excalibur," he said, "and throw it into the lake. Then come back and tell me what you have seen." He lay back, knowing he had not long to live.

Bedivere took Excalibur down to the lake. Then he looked at it. "Why throw away such a beautiful sword?" he thought, so he hid it in the reeds. He went back and told Arthur he had seen nothing unusual.

"You have not done as I asked," said Arthur. "Go back". Bedivere returned, took Excalibur from the reeds and threw it far into the lake. As it fell, a hand rose out of the water, caught it and sank again.

Bedivere ran to tell Arthur what he had seen. "Now help me to the lake before I die," said Arthur. When they reached the shore a barge glided up. In it were four ladies. One was the Lady of the Lake.

Weeping, they laid Arthur in the barge. "Do not mourn me," Arthur said to Bedivere. "I am going to the magic Vale of Avalon to be healed." The barge floated away and Arthur was never seen again.

When Lancelot heard of Mordred's treachery, he sped back to England to fight for Arthur, but he was too late. Heartbroken, he went to see Guinevere. She too was heartbroken and gently refused his offer of protection. She had vowed to live in a convent. Lancelot went to live in a monastery. A few years later Guinevere died. Soon after hearing of her death, Lancelot died too.

Most of the Knights of the Round Table had been killed in battle. The few who still lived went off to fight in the Crusades. And they never met again at Camelot.

No one knew what became of Arthur after the barge carried him away. Some think he was buried at Glastonbury. Others claim that he sleeps in a magic cave in Wales, with the Knights of the Round Table sleeping round him.

Other people say Arthur was taken to the magic Vale of Avalon, where it is always Spring and where everyone is young again. They even say that Arthur still lives there, waiting until England needs him and his knights again.

Copyright © 1989 Usborne Publishing Ltd
First published in 1989 by
Usborne Publishing Ltd
83-85 Saffron Hill,
London EC1N 8RT, England

Printed in Belgium

The material in this book is also published as four separate titles: *The Adventures of Robinson Crusoe, Treasure Island, Gulliver's Travels* and *The Adventures of King Arthur*.

The name Usborne and the device are Trade Marks of Usborne Publishing Ltd.